The Ginghams

THE BACKWARD PICNIC

story by Joan Chase Bowden

illustrated by JoAnne E. Koenig/Creative Studios I, Inc.

For Pamela Rosemary

 GOLDEN PRESS

Western Publishing Company, Inc.
Racine, Wisconsin

One beautiful, sunshiny morning, Sarah made a whole stack of sandwiches, some with jam and some with marmalade.

Then she packed them into her lunch basket and asked, "Who's ready for the picnic?"

The sailor-doll twins, Henry and Harriet, smiled at each other, which meant that *they* were ready.

Barney the dog said, "Woof!" which meant that *he* had been ready since breakfast time!

So Sarah hitched Barney to her little wooden dog-cart. She carefully put the dolls and the lunch basket in the cart. Then off they all went up the road, as fast as they could go, to call for their best friend, Dan.

But what a disappointment! Dan couldn't come with them, after all!

"I'm sorry, Sarah," he said, "but I have too much work to do. My brother Tom has gone to visit our cousin, and I have to take care of the animals."

"You could do your work later," Sarah suggested.

But Dan shook his head. "Our pony's stall needs sweeping right now," he said. "The pigs are thirsty, and the chickens and ducks are hungry. You'll just have to go without me."

Without Dan, they all set out for the picnic grounds at the top of the hill, but Sarah felt fidgety. She didn't want to leave Dan behind, yet she *did* want to have a picnic. She looked at her dolls and at Barney and wondered if they felt fidgety, too.

"Will you have a good time, anyway?" she asked them, looking worried.

Henry smiled, which meant that *he* would.

And Harriet smiled, which meant that *she* would.

But Barney said, "Woof!" which meant that a picnic without Dan would be no fun at all. He pulled the cart slower and s-l-o-w-e-r.

"Land sakes and mercy me!" Grandma Grimble said, standing in her front yard. "What a sad-looking dog! Maybe a piece of my chocolate cake will cheer him up." She hurried right indoors and cut a thick slice for them to share.

Barney felt much happier when he saw Sarah put the cake in the lunch basket. He felt so much happier that he even trotted halfway up the hill!

But by the time they reached the Fletcher farm, Barney began to feel sad again and to go slower and s-l-o-w-e-r.

"Maybe he'd like some of Mother's oatmeal cookies for your picnic," Farmer Fletcher told Sarah.

"Maybe he'd like some of our taffy," said the Johnson family at the next farm.

Other kind neighbors who lived on the hill offered
treats to go into the lunch basket: "Some of our ham?"
"And how about some pie?" "And a few apples?"

It was the slowest journey that Sarah and her dolls had ever made. By the time they reached the picnic grounds at the top of the hill, the dogcart was piled high with good things to eat. But Sarah felt hot and tired—as well as lonely and very sad because she had left Dan behind.

"I wish *he* were here, too," she told Barney, as she unhitched the dog from the cart.

Sarah was so unhappy that she didn't notice when the dogcart began slipping back down the hill. Then she saw her beloved dolls flying down the hillside!

"Help, Barney!" she cried. "We've got to rescue them!" But it was too late.

Faster and faster down the hill rolled the dogcart. Faster and faster ran Sarah and Barney after it.

The cart rolled all the way to the bottom of the hill, and it stopped—WHUMP!—right in the middle of a haystack in Dan's barnyard.

Sarah and Barney were breathless when at last they reached the cart. There were Henry and Harriet, smiling bravely.

It took Sarah a long time to tell Dan what had happened. "Barney was sad, and so was I," she explained. "We missed you. But I think I know now how we can *all* have our picnic."

Then Sarah did what she knew she should have done before. She helped Dan with his work. With *two* doing the chores, they finished in *half* the time.

Soon they were all sitting down—right in Dan's front yard—to the best picnic lunch they had ever tasted.

"This was really a *backward* picnic," said Dan, laughing as he took a second oatmeal cookie.

Sarah agreed happily, "You couldn't come to the picnic, so the picnic came to you! Henry and Harriet and I are *glad!*"

"Woof!" said Barney, which meant that *he* was happy, too, because this was how he had wanted it all the time.